Cameron lived below the high mountains in the ancient
forests of the Scottish Cairngorms. Cameron was a capercaillie,
and capercaillies love to dance.

Cameron's family, the MacFeathers, were the best dancers in the Cairngorms. When Grandad Shaker MacFeather put just one toe on the forest dance floor, everyone stopped to admire him.

Can't-Dance-Cameron

A Scottish Capercaillie Story

Emily Dodd & Katie Pamment

But Cameron hated dancing. When he wiggled,
everyone giggled!

"Why can't I dance?" he whispered to himself.

"You can!" said a voice.

Cameron jumped.

"I'm Hazel," said a red squirrel behind him.

"I've been watching you, and I know you can dance!"

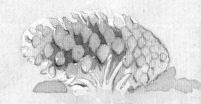

Cameron shook his head. "You've definitely got the wrong bird. I'm Can't-Dance-Cameron MacFeather, the worst dancer in the whole of the Cairngorms."

Hazel smiled to herself. "Cameron," she said, "I've lost my favourite nut. If you help me find it, I'll teach you to dance."

"I'm not very good at finding things," said Cameron, but he followed Hazel down the forest path.

PING!

A pine marten jumped over the path above them and a
branch swung back, showering Cameron in pine needles.

"Oh no!" said Cameron.

"Jump and flutter, and they'll fall off," said Hazel.

So Cameron jumped and fluttered and fluttered and jumped
until he'd shaken off all the pine needles.
They walked on.

CRASH!

A big tree fell across the path in front of them.

"Oh no!" said Cameron.

"There's always a way through," said Hazel. "Duck under the branches: follow me!"

So Cameron ducked and walked and ducked and walked
until he got to the other side of the fallen tree.
"Nice one," said Hazel, and they went on.

WHOOSH!

A wildcat leapt from the undergrowth. She licked her lips.

"Oh no!" whispered Cameron.

"Just don't move. They chase things that move,"
said Hazel, without moving her mouth.

Cameron and Hazel stayed very still.

But Cameron was so scared his knees started knocking together.

The wildcat crouched, ready to pounce…

KICK!

Cameron kicked a pinecone and it flew past
the wildcat, who turned and chased it, bopping
it along with her paw.

"Wow!" said Hazel. "That kick was amazing!"

For the first time in a long time, Cameron smiled.
And he kicked another pinecone, just for fun.

KICK!

"Ah-ha!" said Hazel. "Now I remember where I put my favourite nut. We need to go back to the forest dance floor!"

So Cameron and Hazel went back along the path...

...around the wildcat...

KICK!

DUCK WALK DUCK WALK

…under the CRASHed branches…

…past the pine marten…

PING!

FLUTTER JUMP FLUTTER JUMP

…to the forest dance floor.

Hazel started digging under the tree where they'd met. "Found it!" she cried.

"Sometimes, Cameron, you go looking for something and find that you had it all along."

Hazel smiled to herself. She grabbed a handful of pine needles, threw them over Cameron and shoved him onto the dance floor.

"PING!" she said.

Cameron jumped and fluttered and fluttered and jumped, shaking off the pine needles. He was so angry, he started to make a capercaillie popping noise.

"POP!" "POP!"

When he stopped, Cameron realised there was a circle of birds and animals watching him. He froze. "Oh no!" he whispered.

"CRASH!"

shouted Hazel.

Cameron remembered the fallen tree. He ducked and walked and ducked and walked.

"*Oooh,*" said the capercaillies.

"WHOOSH!" shouted Hazel. Cameron remembered the wildcat and kicked an imaginary pinecone.

KICK!

"*Ahhhh!*" said the crowd. They had never seen a capercaillie kick like that before.
"That's a new move!" boomed Grandad Shaker MacFeather. "That's my grandson!"

"Kick it, Cameron!" everyone cheered.

Cameron kicked again.

He popped, ducked, walked, hopped, jumped and fluttered, and everyone copied his moves. It was the first capercaillie ceilidh of the year, and Cameron was leading the dance!

He winked at Hazel.

"KICK IT, CAMERON!" she shouted.

KICK!